ALY & AJ'S ROCK'N ROLL MYSTERIES
NASHVILLE NIGHTS

by Tracey West and Katherine Noll
illustrated by Aly Michalka

GROSSET & DUNLAP
Published by the Penguin Group
Penguin Group (USA) Inc., 375 Hudson Street, New York, New York 10014, USA
Penguin Group (Canada), 90 Eglinton Avenue East, Suite 700,
Toronto, Ontario M4P 2Y3, Canada
(a division of Pearson Penguin Canada Inc.)
Penguin Books Ltd., 80 Strand, London WC2R 0RL, England
Penguin Group Ireland, 25 St. Stephen's Green, Dublin 2, Ireland
(a division of Penguin Books Ltd.)
Penguin Group (Australia), 250 Camberwell Road, Camberwell, Victoria 3124, Australia
(a division of Pearson Australia Group Pty. Ltd.)
Penguin Books India Pvt. Ltd., 11 Community Centre, Panchsheel Park,
New Delhi—110 017, India
Penguin Group (NZ), 67 Apollo Drive, Rosedale, North Shore 0632, New Zealand
(a division of Pearson New Zealand Ltd.)
Penguin Books (South Africa) (Pty.) Ltd., 24 Sturdee Avenue,
Rosebank, Johannesburg 2196, South Africa

Penguin Books Ltd., Registered Offices:
80 Strand, London WC2R 0RL, England

Cover photo courtesy of Joe Magnani.

Library of Congress Cataloging-in-Publication Data is available.

ISBN 978-0-448-45084-1

CHAPTER ONE:
ENCORE, ENCORE!

"Good night, Nashville," Aly yelled into her microphone. The screaming crowd at the Sommet Center clapped and cheered. Aly grabbed her sister AJ's hand and they ran off the stage together.

"Wow!" AJ panted as she tried to catch her breath. "What a rush!"

"You bet," Aly said as she snagged a bottle of water off of a table. She gulped it down. "But we're not done yet!"

The concert crowd was clamoring for more. *Clap, clap, stomp. Clap, clap, stomp.* The stadium shook as the fans clapped their hands and stomped their feet in rhythm to get Aly and AJ back for one last song.

AJ grabbed Aly's water and took a big swig. "Okay—let's do this!"

The girls raced back onto the stage. The crowd went wild.

"We couldn't leave you all without doing one more song," Aly said into the microphone. "How about this one?"

Aly and AJ nodded to their band. The drummer, Tommy, began tapping out the beat. Matt, the lead guitarist, and Jeffrey, the keyboardist, joined in. Soon the bass player, Malcolm, was playing along. The crowd went wild as they recognized the song "Walking on Sunshine." It was originally recorded back in the 1980s by a band called Katrina and the Waves. Aly and AJ loved it so much they recorded their own version on their album *Into the Rush.*

"I used to think maybe you love me, now baby I'm sure, and I just can't wait till the day when you knock on my door," Aly and AJ sang together.

As they got to the chorus, AJ turned her microphone so it faced the crowd. "We know you know the words—sing it for us!" Aly urged.

"I'm walking on sunshine, and don't it feel good, hey!" The arena echoed as everyone sang the words of the feel-good anthem.

They hit the last note and ran off the stage to thunderous applause.

"I love ending the show with that song," AJ said. "It makes everyone so happy."

Aly smiled. "What a great show! The crowd was so much fun. I love Nashville!"

Their mom, Carrie, and their tour manager, Jim, were waiting for them backstage. Carrie gave them each a big hug.

"Fantastic!" she exclaimed. "You both were

wonderful. I was singing along the entire time!"

Jim smiled. "Everything went off without a hitch. No problems. That's always a good thing," he said.

"You can relax now, Jim," Aly teased. Jim was young and just out of college, but he was very organized and always worried about things running smoothly.

They all walked back into the dressing room. The girls grabbed a couple of bottles of flavored water before flopping on the couch.

"Faith and Hope Walker would like to talk to you," Jim said.

"The new country music singing sister duo?" Aly asked. "They are awesome!"

AJ nodded. "I love their single, 'Nothing Like a Sister.' It's so cool."

"Bring them in, please!" Aly said to Jim. "I can't wait to meet them."

Jim and Carrie left to find Faith and Hope. A minute later, the country music sensations walked through the door.

Faith and Hope were dressed simply, in jeans, boots, and T-shirts, but they both looked beautiful. Faith had long, curly brown hair that fell almost to her waist, and dazzling green eyes. Hope had dark brown hair cut in a sleek bob and the same emerald eyes as her sister. They broke out into huge grins when they saw Aly and AJ.

Faith let out a squeal. "I can't believe it—Aly and AJ right before my very eyes! You all are so talented. I can't believe we're standing in the same room as you!"

Aly and AJ stood up and smiled at the country singer sisters.

"Same goes for us," AJ said. "Mad props on your new single. I've got it on my iPod. It's so sick it's contagious."

"Your show tonight was amazing," Hope said. "And I'm glad you like 'Nothing Like a Sister.' It's the reason why we wanted to talk to you."

Faith nodded. "I know this is short notice, but

we would love for you both to be in the video for the song. I don't know how long you plan to be in town for, but we're going to be shooting tomorrow. We need to have the video done by next Sunday night for the National Music Awards. It's going to premiere then."

"Wow, that's a big deal," AJ said. Practically everybody in the country tuned in to the National Music Awards every year to watch singers and bands get honored for their songs and CDs. The hottest acts in music gave live performances between awards. And every year, the show aired a video from one up-and-coming act. Faith and Hope were lucky to have been chosen. Millions of people would see their video.

"Since the song is all about sisters, we decided to invite other sister music acts to be in the video with us," Hope added. "It would be real amazing if you two could do it."

Aly and AJ looked at each other, and their sister intuition kicked in. They both knew what the other was thinking.

"We would love to be in your video," Aly said with a big grin on her face. "It sounds like a lot of fun. Are any other sister acts besides us in the video?"

Faith's eyes sparkled mischievously. "We're waiting to hear from two really famous sisters. I'd tell you, but I don't want to jinx it. Plus, if they agree, it'll be a real surprise."

"Ooh, I like surprises," Aly said. She looked at AJ. "What do you say?"

"I love the idea of a sister-themed video," AJ answered. "We don't have to leave for our gig until Sunday, so we've got almost a whole week to spend here anyway. Let's go for it!"

Faith clapped her hands together. "Wonderful!" she exclaimed. "We'll give all the details to Jim."

"Now how about letting us take you out for dinner tonight?" Hope asked. "When you come to Nashville, you've got to try some hot chicken!"

"Hot like hot in temperature, or hot and spicy?" Aly asked.

"Hot and spicy!" Faith said. "And we know the best place for it."

"I don't know," AJ said apprehensively. "Spicy doesn't always agree with me."

Hope laughed as she linked her arm through AJ's. "Don't worry—they've got mild, too. Let's go. You'll love Nashville at night!"

CHAPTER TWO:
SISTER SENSATIONS

"Music Row!" Jim said as he drove Aly and AJ through Nashville the next morning. "The home of country music."

AJ looked up from the guidebook of Nashville she was reading. "It says here that Music Row is the heart of Nashville's music industry. It is home to record labels, recording studios, video production houses, and radio stations," she said.

Aly took a large gulp from the coffee she was

holding in her hand. "I need caffeine this morning. We got to bed a little late, although I'm glad we went out with Faith and Hope."

"We have so much in common," AJ said. "They've both been singing since they were little, just like us. And we like a lot of the same music, too. It will be a blast to shoot this video with them."

Aly nodded. "I know we just met them, but it's like we've known them forever, right?"

Jim pulled up to a large brick building. The sign on the front read NASHVILLE STAR STUDIOS.

"This is the place," Jim said. "I'll pick you guys up later. Have fun!"

Aly and AJ hopped out of the car and were greeted by Faith and Hope, who had walked out to welcome them.

"Hey!" Faith called. "Long time no see!"

"We are going to have so much fun today," Hope said as she gave Aly and AJ a hug. "Let me show you where we are filming. The studio is huge—it's like a maze!"

Just then, a large black limousine pulled up behind Jim's car. A chauffeur wearing a black suit and hat sprung out of the driver's side and walked around the car to the rear passenger door. He opened it with a flourish, and three tall, beautiful young women stepped out of the car. They all looked a lot alike, with their long brown hair, dark skin, and high cheekbones.

Aly grabbed AJ's sleeve and tugged. "Do you know who that is?" she hissed in a loud whisper. "It's HeavenSent!"

AJ recognized the sister group right away. The R & B singers were superhot. Last month their single "Spotlight" had hit number one. AJ wondered if the sisters were going to be in Faith and Hope's video. But instead of walking toward Nashville Star, they turned and headed for the building next door. They disappeared inside as the girls watched.

"Wow!" Aly said. "Holly, Sabrina, and Eve in person. I've seen so much of them on TV and in magazines the last few months. Hey—they're a sister group! Did you ask them to be in your video?"

Hope nodded. "We did, but they refused. They said they were busy shooting their own video."

"From what I've heard, HeavenSent is one of the hardest working groups in the business. It seems all they do is practice, tour, record, and do publicity," AJ said.

"Sometimes it seems like that's all we do, too," Aly pointed out.

"Right, but you need to make time for other things, too," Hope said. "If I didn't see my friends and family every few weeks, I'd be too sad to sing."

"True," Aly agreed. "And a little chill time now and then is important, too. I mean, we're musicians, but we're people, too."

"Well, whatever HeavenSent is doing, it's working," Faith chimed in. "I'm sure they'll clean up at the National Music Awards. I've heard they're very competitive."

"Let's get going," Hope said. "Lionel is eager to get started. He's the video director."

Aly and AJ followed Faith and Hope inside the studio building. They walked through a maze of hallways until they came to the soundstage where the video would be shot. It was a huge room with a high ceiling that had a network of lights hanging from it. A balding man with a beard was holding a clipboard as he talked into a phone. When he saw Faith and Hope approaching, he smiled and ended his call.

"You must be Aly and AJ," he said. He held out his hand. "I'm Lionel, the video director. It's great to be working with you."

Aly and AJ both shook his hand as they said hello.

"And I'm sure you'll want to meet the other sisters appearing in the video," Lionel said. "Let me introduce you to Cadence and Calista."

AJ and Aly looked at each other, their eyes wide and their mouths open.

"Cadence and Calista Collins are here?" AJ asked in disbelief.

Faith let out a giggle. "We wanted to surprise you. They're in town for a month, recording a new album. Isn't it great that they agreed to do the video?"

"Great—it's awesome!" Aly chimed in. "We loved their TV show when we were little." She began to sing. *"Welcome to the Fun House. We're gonna laugh and giggle the day away."*

AJ rolled her eyes. "Oh, no. Now she'll be singing the theme song to *Fun House* all day! But seriously, we watched that show every Friday night."

"We did, too," Hope said, smiling. "All of America did. Imagine growing up on TV like that? I think they were six when they started the show, and it lasted for ten years."

AJ nodded. "They were so funny on that show. And when they started their music career—remember how we bugged Mom to get us their album?"

Aly laughed. "I promised to do the dishes for a month!"

"It's amazing how they transformed their careers," Hope said. "They started out as child stars, then formed one of the hottest pop duos around. They're on a different magazine cover every week. I couldn't believe it when they agreed to do the video with us."

"It blew my mind," Faith agreed. "We're really lucky. Not only are they megastar sisters, but they're twins, too. This video is going to be fantastic."

"*Twin*tastic!" Aly said. "Remember—that's what Cadence and Calista used to say on *Fun House*."

AJ chuckled. "I sure do. I can't believe we're going to finally meet them!"

Lionel smiled at the girls' excitement. "Come with me and we'll make your dreams come true!"

He led Aly and AJ toward the far wall of the soundstage as Hope and Faith went to get into costume. Two chairs were placed against the wall. In one chair sat a woman in her late twenties with a sleek blond bob with bangs cut in a straight line right over her eyes. She was talking on her pink cell phone. Next to her sat a woman who looked to be around the same age and build. She had her long blond hair pulled back into a ponytail and wore large, dark sunglasses and a baseball cap.

"Excuse me, Calista, Cadence. I'd like to introduce you to Aly and AJ. They'll be appearing in the video today, too," Lionel said. "This is Calista." He gestured toward the girl wearing the baseball cap. "And this is Cadence."

Cadence gave a curt nod. She was still talking on the phone. In a quiet voice, Calista said, "Hi."

"I've got to get back to work," Lionel said. "I'll let you guys chat. We'll let you know when your scenes will be shot." He walked off.

Aly was so excited that the words just poured out of her. "Until Cadence got her hair cut, it was so easy to get you two mixed up—I mean you look so much alike. You even have identical heart-shaped birthmarks, right? On your shoulders? I know all this because I used to get your fan club newsletter. I'm sorry, I must be totally babbling!"

Cadence let out a sigh. "I'll have to call you back," she said into her cell phone. She looked at Aly, and it wasn't in a friendly way. "I'm sorry, what did you say?"

Aly blushed. "I'm sorry; I know I was going on and on. It's just we loved your show so much. It's really a thrill to meet you both."

"Thanks," Cadence said. But she didn't smile or say anything else, and Calista just sat next to her, not saying a word.

AJ tried to break the silence. "Calista, I loved the dress you wore to that movie premiere a couple of months ago. You know, the one that you said you designed yourself? It was so pretty."

Calista looked over at her sister.

"Listen," Cadence said. "I don't mean to be rude, but Calista isn't feeling well right now. So if you don't mind, we'd really like some privacy."

AJ was taken aback. "Uh, okay, of c-course," she stammered. "Aly, let's go."

Aly and AJ walked away from the sisters. When they were out of earshot, AJ said to Aly, "That didn't go so well."

Aly frowned. "It was certainly *not* twintastic!"

CHAPTER THREE:
IT'S A WRAP!

"I know Cadence said she didn't mean to be rude, but she sure was good at it," Aly remarked. She and AJ sat in makeup, getting prepped for the shoot.

"We were definitely dissed," AJ agreed. "Maybe it was because Calista wasn't feeling well."

Aly sighed. "I guess. It's just that when I was little, I dreamed about meeting Calista and Cadence. I never thought it would be like this!"

Tina, the woman applying their makeup, looked up from her brushes and bottles.

"Calista and Cadence? I was surprised to learn they would be here today," she said. "Rumor has it that those two are not getting along. In fact, I heard that they canceled two shows earlier this month."

AJ looked thoughtful. "Maybe they're just going through a tough time. We should try to be more understanding, Aly, and not let it bother us."

"You're right. I won't take it personally that my childhood idols totally dissed me," Aly said.

Tina swirled the makeup brush one last time over AJ's face. "All finished!" she said.

AJ stood up and smoothed down her skirt. It was a cute brown corduroy skirt with a side zipper and a pretty flower embellishment with sequins on the front left. She wore it with a vintage three-quarter length sleeve white lace top and platform boots with vintage crystals on the heels.

Aly was wearing a black camisole top that was

trimmed with lace and had a cute ruffle accent down the front. She also wore a pair of vintage-looking, five-pocket bootleg faded jeans and high-heeled black boots.

The premise of their part of the video, Lionel had explained to them after their disastrous meeting with Calista and Cadence, was that Aly and AJ were each on a horrible date. AJ leaves her date and rescues Aly, and the two go off to see Faith and Hope in concert.

Part of the studio was transformed into the inside of a restaurant. The set looked very realistic, with tables covered in cream brocade tablecloths and a faux wall that was sponge-painted a rich red with cream accents.

AJ laughed out loud when she met Michael, the handsome model who was playing her date. The makeup crew and costume people had decked him out to look like a total nerd. His hair was slicked down with grease and parted in the middle, except for one long strand that stood straight up on the top of his head. He wore thick-rimmed glasses, a white button-up shirt, and suspenders on pants that were pulled up practically to his chest.

Michael grinned at AJ. "Meet your dream date!"

"I never judge a book by its cover," AJ told him. "But in this case, I just might!"

Lionel directed AJ and Michael to take their places. They were supposed to pretend to eat dinner. AJ tries to be nice, but Michael does some funny things, like blowing his nose into the cloth dinner napkin and spilling his drink all over AJ. She then goes into the bathroom and climbs out the window to escape the horrible date.

Michael was very funny, and Lionel had to stop filming a few times because AJ was laughing when she was supposed to look disgusted. Finally, they got the perfect take and Aly was up next.

Aly was shooting on a set that looked like a park. A backdrop that looked like rolling green hills and a blue sky was behind her. She had to pretend to be on a picnic with her date, a handsome actor named Brady. Aly had to sit on a blanket across from Brady and try to talk to him, but instead Brady pulls out a mirror to look at himself and flex his muscles. She takes his mirror away and instead he checks himself out in a spoon. Just when Aly's had enough, AJ comes, grabs her sister by the hand, and the two run off together, just as the chorus of the song "Nothing Like a Sister" begins to play.

"That was so much fun," AJ said to Aly. "Michael was so funny!"

"Brady did a great job of acting like a conceited jerk," Aly said. "And he seems like such a nice guy, too."

As the production crew was setting up for Cadence and Calista's scenes, Aly and AJ sat in chairs on the sidelines to watch. Lionel was going over the scene with the girls.

Aly pulled her sketchbook out of her purse.

"This will be a good way to pass the time. I haven't had a chance to draw in ages!"

"I'm interested to see what Cadence and Calista will be doing," AJ said as she watched. The girls wore adorable sundresses and cute wedge sandals. Their set was constructed to look like a street filled with fancy stores. Cadence and Calista were both holding lots of shopping bags. The idea, Lionel said, was that they get so caught up in shopping that they are late for Faith and Hope's concert.

Filming started. Cadence and Calista walked down the street set, chatting and smiling. Calista looked very '50s glamorous, wearing a scarf on her head, big sunglasses, and a white pearl-buttoned sweater over her dress. Cadence's head was bare, but she still looked very sophisticated. Lionel was telling Calista to look at her watch while juggling all the shopping bags. She lifted her arm up, but the sweater was covering the watch.

"Calista, can you please take the sweater off

and we'll film that again?" Lionel asked. Calista nodded and removed her sweater.

They shot the scene again. Aly was having a blast sketching her childhood idols.

"Cut!" a voice called. But it wasn't Lionel. Aly looked up from her sketchbook.

It was Cadence. She had walked off the set and picked up Calista's sweater.

"I'm worried Calista will catch a chill," Cadence said. "She hasn't been feeling well, you know. I don't think she should risk her health just for a music video."

AJ leaned over to Aly. "If she's so sick, why didn't she just stay home today?" she whispered.

Lionel remained polite. "Of course," he said smoothly. "Don't worry about it. I've got enough footage without the sweater, so it's no problem."

Cadence and Calista were done, and Faith and Hope were now on set to film their concert scene. The idea was that the country music singers were performing in a small Nashville club.

Faith and Hope took to the stage. Lionel planned to film the sisters performing the entire song from start to finish, and intersperse it with the footage of Aly, AJ, Cadence, and Calista.

Faith and Hope stood in front of their microphones. The music had just begun to play when a loud shout interrupted it.

Lionel sighed. "What's going on?" he asked.

"I'll tell you what's going on." A man strode onto the set, followed by an angry-looking security guard. "I need to talk to Faith and Hope now!"

The man wore a three-piece business suit. He had sandy brown hair and horn-rimmed glasses.

The security guard grabbed his arm. "You have to leave, sir," he said firmly.

"You can't just fire me as your manager," the man yelled at Faith and Hope, ignoring the guard. "We had a contract. I can sue you! This entire video was my idea, too. In fact, without me no one would even know the names Faith and Hope. I created you!" He took a deep breath and was getting ready to say more when another security guard appeared. The two guards dragged the man off of the set.

"I'm so glad he's out of here," Hope said. She looked pale and shaken. Faith didn't look much better.

Lionel called for a break. Aly and AJ went to comfort their new friends.

"That was Parker Mackenzie, our former manager," Faith explained. "He was with us from the beginning of our career. But in the last year or so he's been making really bad decisions, really hurting our career."

"That's an understatement," Holly said. "He's a real hothead. He blew up at the head of our record company for no good reason and almost lost us our contract with them. Luckily, we have a great attorney who was able to help us get out of our contract with Parker, fair and square. We fired him a few days ago.

He wasn't happy and keeps threatening to sue us."

"We have to make sure he doesn't get back on the set," Hope said. "We don't need him causing any more scenes!"

Aly slipped her arm around Faith. "Don't worry about it—after that stunt he'll never get back in here."

Faith and Hope were feeling better, so filming started up again. The final scene was a lot of fun. Aly and AJ and Cadence and Calista joined the scene at the concert. They grooved out to the tune about sisters.

"It's a wrap!" Lionel exclaimed. "Thanks, everybody. It looks like this video is a real winner!"

The crew cheered. Everyone mingled and chatted before leaving. Aly and AJ decided to give it one final try with Cadence and Calista.

"It was nice meeting you," AJ said.

"Yes, you too," Cadence said. Calista smiled and nodded.

"Thank you guys so much," Hope said as she and Faith joined them. "We would love to thank you by taking you all out for dinner. What do you say?"

"We need to get home," Cadence said. "But thanks anyway. Good night everyone." The pop duo headed for the door.

"You know we would love to go," Aly said.

"We had such a good time last night," AJ added. "And it feels like we've known you guys forever."

Faith smiled. "I'm so glad you feel that way, because we feel the same way about you both. It's like we're old friends."

"So where should we head to tonight?" Hope asked.

"I know the coolest club on Cannery Row," Faith said. "We can get a bite to eat and listen to some really great local bands at the same time."

"Sounds awesome!" Aly said. "Let's go."

The club, Virtue, was a laid-back space with hardwood floors and '50s-style vinyl couches and chairs against the walls. The girls sat around the S-shaped vinyl bar in the center of the club and munched on pub-style food as they listened to three different bands. The music was rock with a country edge. Aly and AJ spent a lot of the time laughing and joking with Faith and Hope.

"Wow! Look at the time," AJ said with a glance at her watch. "I'm beat. I think it's time to head back to the hotel and get some rest."

"We'll have to get together again before you guys leave town," Faith said.

"I think I want you both to move to Nashville!" Hope cried.

Aly and AJ said good night and returned to the hotel. After they each took a quick shower, they got into bed.

"As soon as I put my head on this pillow, I'll be out like a light," Aly joked.

After a long and busy day, they both quickly fell asleep. But the phone suddenly began ringing and jolted them awake.

Aly fumbled for the phone on the nightstand. "Hello?" she said groggily.

"Aly? It's Faith." She sounded upset. "I'm sorry to bother you, but someone has stolen the tape of the video shoot!"

CHAPTER FOUR:
THE CLUE IN THE CONTROL ROOM

Aly felt wide awake now. "Faith, that's awful! Are you okay?"

Faith took a deep breath. "I . . . I think so," she said. "I don't mean to bother you. It's just . . . we don't know what to do!"

"Are you sure the tape was stolen?" Aly asked. "What happened, exactly?"

AJ was wide awake now, too. She leaned close to the phone to hear what Faith was saying.

"Lionel called us," Faith said. "After we left, he took a dinner break. He locked up the tape in the control room. When he got back, the control room door was wide open, and the tape was gone."

Faith's voice broke, and she started to cry.

"Oh, Faith, I'm so sorry!" Aly said. "There should be a backup of the tape, shouldn't there?"

"Lionel said both copies were taken," Faith replied, panic rising in her voice. The words started to pour out of her. "That means we can't show the video at the awards show. This was our big chance to really make it, and now it's over! I don't even know if we'd have time to make another one, because it's already Tuesday morning, and the show is on Sunday. Besides, the record company will never give us the money to film another one!"

Faith started to cry again.

"Where are you now?" asked Aly.

"Hope and I are back at the studio," Faith replied. "Our new manager, Maxine, came down, too. She's trying to figure out what to do."

"AJ and I will be there as quickly as we can," Aly promised, glancing at the clock. It was almost three o'clock in the morning.

She hung up the phone. AJ shook her head. "Wow, that's terrible! They definitely need some moral support right now. I'll wake up Jim."

Fifteen minutes later they were in Jim's rented car, heading for the studio. Jim gave a yawn.

"I was having the nicest dream," he said, sighing.

"Sorry, Jim," AJ said. "Faith and Hope have been really nice to us. And they reached out to us, too."

"You're helping us do a good deed," Aly added.

Jim grinned. "I should know by now that you two can't turn your back on someone who needs help," he said. "I am happy to be your humble servant."

Aly and AJ laughed. "We couldn't ask for a better one," AJ said.

About a block away from the studio, Jim let out a low whistle.

"Check out that car," he said, nodding at a red sports car on the side of the road. He even slowed down a little. "Sweet! That's a limited edition from Italy. I've never seen one in person before, only in pictures. Man, I'd like to get behind the wheel of that baby."

"Come on, you know our Hello Kitty bus is a much cooler ride," Aly joked.

"She's a beauty, but sometimes a guy has a need for speed," Jim replied.

They had reached Nashville Star Studios. Faith and Hope were standing outside the door, along with a woman in a turquoise pantsuit. Her brown hair was teased high and held in place with lots of hairspray.

Faith rushed toward them. "Aly, AJ, thank

you!" she said. "I feel kind of silly now for calling you. I mean, we just met."

"We're glad you called," Aly replied. "What can we do to help?"

"First, meet Maxine, our new manager," Faith said, leading Aly and AJ to the woman with the teased hair.

"Nice to meet you," AJ said.

"It's a pleasure to meet you two lovely girls as well," Maxine said, speaking with a deep Southern drawl. "It was so nice of you to agree to be in the video."

"Is it really stolen?" Aly asked.

Maxine nodded. "I'm afraid so."

"Have you called the police?" AJ asked.

"My dear, Lionel and I agreed not to take such drastic measures," Maxine said. "It's nasty business, and I don't want Faith and Hope to get caught up in it. We're hoping to find a solution in time for the awards show without involving the police at all."

The manager looked at her watch. "I'm going inside to talk to Lionel. Y'all try not to worry, okay?"

Faith and Hope nodded, but they both looked tired and upset.

"I just don't know why someone would want to steal our tape," Hope said. "It's a real mystery."

Aly and AJ looked at each other. Since the *Insomniatic* tour had started, they had stumbled across one mystery after another. They were beginning to feel more like detectives than musicians. In New York City, they had helped recover stolen guitars from the Girls Rock Academy. In Miami, they'd met a fashion designer who was a victim of sabotage and helped her find the culprit. And they had just come from judging a songwriting contest in Seattle, where one of the competitors had resorted to dirty tricks to ruin the contest.

Aly and AJ had kept their sleuthing quiet, for the most part. Most people would think it was strange. But the sisters felt they could trust Faith and Hope.

"This is going to sound weird, but Aly and I have gotten pretty good at solving mysteries lately," AJ said. "Maybe we can try to help."

"Oh, that would be so nice!" Faith said.

"We'll take all the help we can get," Hope added. "The awards show is only on Sunday. We need to figure something out by then."

"We'll do our best," AJ promised. "Do you think we can look inside the studio?"

"Sure," Faith replied.

The girls all walked inside. Maxine was inside a glass-windowed office, talking with Lionel.

"Which one is the control room?" AJ asked.

Hope pointed to a door on the far wall. "Over there."

As they approached the room, Aly and AJ saw that the door was open.

"Lionel swears he locked it," Faith said. "Somebody must have unlocked it. Maybe someone with a key."

"Or they might have picked the lock," Aly said, bending down to pick something up off of the floor. When she stood back up, she was holding a small, silver piece of metal. The end was bent so it almost looked like a letter L.

"That looks like a lock pick," AJ said.

Aly jiggled the door knob. "This lock would probably be easy to pick."

"And if the person who opened the door used a lock pick, that means they didn't have a key," AJ said. "So that probably rules out anyone who works for the studio. We can ask Lionel to be sure."

"So it was an outside job," Hope said. She smiled a little. "Hey, this is just like a crime show on TV or something. What should we do with the evidence?"

"I'll hold on to it," Aly said. "If Maxine decides to call in the police, we can give it to them."

"We should look around some more," AJ suggested.

"I'll take the control room," Aly offered.

AJ nodded. "I'll look around the rest of the studio."

AJ scanned the room. There were two ways to get in from outside—the front entrance and a side entrance. If the thief had dropped any clues, they would most likely have dropped them on the path from one of the doors to the control room.

AJ started at the front door and walked slowly to the control room, her eyes on the floor. She didn't see anything unusual.

Then she started at the control room and walked toward the side door. A few feet from the door, something caught her eye—something glittery. She reached down and picked it up.

It was a pin, shaped like angel wings, and set with diamonds. AJ recognized the logo right away.

It was the symbol for the popular R & B sister group, HeavenSent!

CHAPTER FIVE:
HEAVENLY SUSPECTS

AJ heard Aly's voice behind her.

"Find anything?"

AJ quickly put the pin in her pocket and turned around. Faith and Hope stood behind Aly.

"No," AJ lied. "How about you?"

"Nothing," Aly said. "I think the lock pick is our best clue."

"It's a start," AJ said. She yawned. "I forgot how late it is. Faith and Hope, are you going to be okay?"

The sisters nodded. "We'll be fine," Faith said. "Thanks so much for coming here. It's strange, but I have a feeling you two are here to help us. Like guardian angels, almost."

"We definitely don't have wings," Aly said. "But we'll do what we can to help. We'll call you in the morning, okay?"

Faith nodded. "Thanks again."

Aly and AJ headed back outside to the car, where Jim was waiting for them. They got inside, and Jim drove off.

AJ leaned over to Aly, who sat in the front passenger seat.

"Aly, I lied," she said. "I did find something." She showed Aly the diamond angel pin.

"That's the HeavenSent logo!" Aly exclaimed.

AJ nodded. "I know. That's why I didn't say anything in front of Faith and Hope. Just because there's a clue doesn't mean someone is guilty. That's happened to us before. Faith and Hope were pretty upset. I didn't want them to go calling up HeavenSent in the middle of the night."

"Smart thinking," Aly said. "This is exciting. Why would HeavenSent want to steal the tape?"

AJ yawned again. "Can we talk about this in the morning? I'm beat."

Jim shook his head. "You know, you girls might not talk to me about this whole detective thing you're doing, but don't think I haven't noticed. You're not going to leave the music business to become detectives are you? I mean, if you did, I'd still stick with you. I always thought I'd make a great private eye. But I think your fans would miss you."

Now Aly was yawning, too. "Jim, I didn't hear a word you just said. My brain is mush." She closed her eyes and leaned back in her seat.

"Fine. Be mysterious, then," Jim said.

Aly and AJ slept until ten o'clock Tuesday

morning. They ate a late breakfast at Wally's Waffles, a small restaurant down the street from their hotel. Aly was digging into a plate of strawberry waffles with whipped cream, while AJ had chosen the Southern pecan waffles with maple syrup.

"These are waffle-icious!" AJ joked.

"Definitely!" Aly agreed. "I'm feeling wide awake now, too. Although it's probably the sugar rush."

AJ took her notebook from her bag. "Now that we're fueled up, we should really talk about what happened last night," she said. "I want to make some notes. Let's talk about the facts. What do we know?"

"We know that the tape was stolen when Lionel was at dinner," Aly said. "Faith told me that was between 7:30 and 8:30 at night."

AJ wrote that down. "Got it. We also know that the tape was locked in the control room, and whoever took it used a lock pick to open the door. That reminds me—we need to ask Jim if the studio engineers have a key to the studio. If they do, we can probably rule them out."

"Right," Aly said. "Then there's that pin you found." She took a copy of *Note* magazine from her bag. Then she turned to a page that showed a picture of the angel-shaped pin next to a photo of HeavenSent.

"I remembered reading about this," Aly continued. "The diamond pins were a special gift from their record company after their last record went platinum. They were specially made—so the pin has to belong to either Sabrina, Holly, or Eve."

"Right," AJ agreed. "We know the sisters were recording at the studio next door yesterday. So one of them would have had the opportunity to break into the studio. I just can't figure out why they would want to steal Faith and Hope's tape."

Aly turned to another page in *Note*, a full-page ad for the National Music Awards. "HeavenSent is performing live at the awards," Aly said.

"Faith said that the sisters in HeavenSent are very competitive," AJ chimed in. "They knew Faith and Hope's video was going to premiere at the awards. Maybe they didn't want the country-singing sisters to steal their own sister limelight."

"That makes total sense," Aly agreed.

"So that means that HeavenSent had the opportunity, *and* a motive," AJ added.

"They're not the only ones with a motive," Aly said. "Remember Faith and Hope's old manager, Parker something? He was super angry about the video. I was thinking he might have stolen the video just to get revenge on them."

AJ nodded and wrote quickly in her notebook. "That's a totally great motive," she said. "Good thinking."

"So what now?" Aly asked.

"I think we need to interview our suspects," AJ replied. "Let's start with HeavenSent first. That pin is the best clue we have."

"You're right, but how do we get close to them? They're super famous," Aly said. "Unless . . ."

AJ was already dialing her cell phone. "I'm sure Jim can help us."

Aly laughed. "We're going to have to make him our official detective assistant."

Fondue

CHAPTER SIX:
A MYSTERIOUS NOTE

"Jim is a miracle worker," Aly said as she and AJ rode in a cab to Nashville Star Studios. "First, he called Lionel and found out about the keys. Lionel says his studio guys have keys, so the thief is probably somebody from outside the studio. Then he actually got us a meeting with HeavenSent!"

"I just wish we were meeting them under better circumstances," AJ said. She put her hand in her pocket and closed her fingers around the HeavenSent pin. "I wonder how the pin ended up at the scene of the crime?"

"Hopefully, we'll find out," Aly said as the cab pulled up in front of the studios.

Faith and Hope were standing outside, talking to Lionel. AJ paid the cab driver and thanked her.

"Aly, AJ," Faith's face lit up when she spotted them. "It's so good to see you guys. We've got some good news and some bad news."

"The good news," Hope said. "Is that our record company has given us the okay to reshoot the video."

Lionel frowned. "But Cadence and Calista have refused to do a reshoot. The producers of the National Music Awards wanted to premiere the video when they heard Cadence and Calista would be in it. They've been trying to get them to perform on the awards for years, so for them this was the next best thing. I'm not sure if they'll play the video if Cadence and Calista aren't in it."

"Maxine is talking to the producers about it now," Faith said. "But if you guys aren't in it either, then I doubt we have a chance."

"Of course, we'll help out in any way we can," AJ assured them.

"If you decide to reshoot, we'll be there and be ready!" Aly said. "But why won't Cadence and Calista do the video again?"

Hope shrugged. "The excuse is that Calista still isn't feeling well. Physically, she seemed fine when they were here. But there was something strange going on. I guess the rumors about the sisters not getting along are true."

"Let us know when you need us, and we'll be there," AJ told them. "But we've got to get to a meeting now."

After Faith and Hope promised to call them to let them know about the video reshoot, Aly and AJ headed toward the same studio they saw HeavenSent enter the other day.

"Jim said they were still filming today," Aly said. "And that they would be happy to meet us."

After giving their names to a security guard sitting at the front desk, Aly and AJ were escorted through the building to a soundstage very similar to the one they had been on yesterday. Lights and cameras hung from the ceiling. This set was made to look like a fancy red carpet event. But no one was filming. Instead, Holly, Sabrina, and Eve were sitting on the sidelines, taking a break.

The three sisters were dressed in glamorous gowns that were truly breathtaking. Holly wore a sparkling sleeveless sheath that was covered with crystals. Her long, dark hair was parted to one side and fell over her shoulder in a tumble of curls. Sabrina wore her hair up in a French twist. It looked perfect with her elegant, white silk, empire-waist gown that was embellished with a black velvet bow. Eve wore a black, floor-length dress that had a jeweled neckline.

"Hi," Aly said as she and AJ walked over to the sister group. "I'm Aly. This is my sister AJ. It's so nice to meet you. By the way, I love your dresses. You all look so amazing!"

The sisters smiled at Aly and AJ. "Thank you," Sabrina said. "The concept for our video is a big red carpet event. That's why we are all decked out. I'm Sabrina, and this is Holly and Eve," she said as she gestured to her sisters.

Aly and AJ greeted the girls.

"Thanks for agreeing to meet with us," AJ said. "We heard you were shooting next door, and we've always admired your music."

Aly chimed in. "We spent all day yesterday helping Faith and Hope with their new video. But someone stole the footage!"

The sisters' smiles changed to serious looks. Holly nodded. "We heard about that. It's such a shame!"

"I can't imagine working so hard on something

and then having someone come along and take it," Eve said. "We're going to be extra careful on this set with our video footage. It would be a shame for it all to go to waste."

AJ reached into her pocket. "I think this belongs to one of you," she said. She opened her hand and showed the pin to HeavenSent. "We found it in the studio last night after the break-in was discovered."

Holly, Sabrina, and Eve exchanged puzzled glances with one another. Sabrina reached out and took the pin from AJ.

"Thank you," she said as AJ dropped the pin into her hand. "I don't know how that got there. It isn't mine. Holly, Eve, does this belong to either of you?"

Holly and Eve shook their heads no. There was an awkward silence for a moment. It was clear that Aly and AJ were wondering why the pin would have been found in the studio where the video footage was stolen.

"It's probably a cheap copy," Holly suggested.

"People are always copying our style," Sabrina added. She slipped the pin into her purse.

"It must be a great copy, then, because those look like real diamonds to me," AJ said.

None of the sisters had an answer for that. There was an awkward silence.

Aly decided to try and change the subject. "So what song is this video for?"

Sabrina looked relieved to have something else to talk about. "It's for our newest single, 'Sister Power.'"

Aly and AJ exchanged glances. Faith and Hope's video was sister-themed, too!

But before they had a chance to ask more questions, a production assistant interrupted them.

"Girls, we're ready to resume shooting," he said to HeavenSent.

Holly, Eve, and Sabrina stood up. All three were very tall to begin with, but in their ultra-high heels they towered over Aly and AJ.

"Thanks for stopping by," Sabrina said.

"Good luck with the video!" Aly replied. They said their good-byes and walked into the hallway.

Aly looked at AJ. "What did you think of that?" she asked.

AJ glanced around. "We'd better not talk here. Besides, I'm getting hungry. We can talk it over at lunch."

They began to walk toward the entrance when Holly came into the hallway.

"Excuse me," she said as she teetered by them on her high heels. She stumbled and bumped into Aly, clinging to her for a second before she steadied herself.

"Sorry about that," Holly said. "I'm just trying to find the bathroom. These heels can be hard to navigate in."

"No problem," Aly said.

"Nice meeting you both. Good-bye," Holly said. Then she turned and made her way down the hall.

"Every time I see a picture of HeavenSent, they're always in heels," AJ remarked thoughtfully. "Why would Holly have trouble walking in them now?"

"Mmmm, hot, melty, cheesy goodness." AJ was in heaven as she speared a chunk of bread with her fork and dipped it into the bubbling cheese fondue. She and Aly had decided to go to a fondue restaurant for lunch. They sat at a booth that had its very own tabletop fondue pot. Inside was the melted cheese, and Aly and AJ were dipping bread and veggies into it. It was delicious!

Aly crunched on a piece of broccoli covered in cheese. "This was a great idea!"

AJ patted her guidebook, which was sitting on the table next to her. "It's good to have one of these. I like to get one for every city we visit."

"So, what did you think of HeavenSent?" Aly asked.

AJ shook her head as she dipped another piece of bread into the fondue. "I'm not sure. They seemed perfectly nice, but they weren't exactly chatty."

"They were very closed-mouthed about the pin, that's for sure," Aly said. "No one wanted to say anything about it."

"I'm pretty sure those diamonds were real, and that pin wasn't a copy. I wish we could get a good look at it, but Sabrina kept it," AJ said, frowning.

"I thought that was a little suspicious," Aly remarked. "Do you think the pin was hers?"

"I don't know," AJ answered, sighing. "At least the meeting wasn't a total waste. What did you think of the fact that HeavenSent's new single and video is sister-themed, just like Faith and Hope's?"

"I think it adds to their motive," Aly replied. "Faith and Hope's video is supposed to premiere at the music awards. HeavenSent are performing there. Let's say they stole the footage to keep Faith and Hope from stealing their spotlight. It makes more sense now. If both groups come out with sister-themed videos, they'll be compared against each other."

"Even though it was under weird circumstances, it still was amazing to meet HeavenSent in person," AJ said. "They are so pretty—and did you see those dresses?"

"I would have loved to sketch them," Aly replied. "In fact, I'd like to do a few rough sketches while I can still remember."

She grabbed her bag and reached inside for her sketchpad. But instead her fingers closed around a folded piece of paper. She pulled it out of the bag.

"What's this?" she wondered. She opened the note and began to read it.

"Please meet me at Club Constellation at midnight tonight. Holly," Aly read. She looked up at AJ. "You were right. Holly can walk just fine in heels. She must have used them as an excuse so she could bump into me and slip this note in my bag!"

AJ grabbed the note and read it herself.

"Do you think the pin is Holly's?" Aly asked her.

"I don't know, but I think we're going to find out!" AJ said.

CHAPTER SEVEN:
MIDNIGHT DETECTING

"I can't wait to find out why Holly wants to meet us," Aly said to AJ. The two stood in front of Club Constellation, the most exclusive, hottest club in town. When celebrities came to town, this was where they went. Aly and AJ knew the club was dressy, so they ditched their jeans and put on some new dresses they had bought on tour. AJ wore a black velour dress with cute little flutter sleeves and a crocheted, yoke-style neckline. Aly dressed in a cream-colored brocade halter dress with a ruffled hem.

It was 11:30 at night. The girls wanted to get to the club early so they could check out the club before Holly showed up. A crowd of people was lined up outside the door, waiting to get in. Everyone in the young crowd was dressed to impress; the girls favored minidresses and high heels, while a lot of the boys wore pin-striped pants and jackets. Aly and AJ were glad they had changed.

The bouncer at the door smiled when Aly and AJ approached. "I heard Aly and AJ were in town!" he exclaimed. "I'm glad you decided to visit us. Come right in."

He held the door open for them. Some members of the crowd looked at them enviously as they walked into the dark club. The ceiling was pitch-black, but tiny lights dotted it, making it look like the night sky. The lights twinkled and glowed. In the middle of the room was a dance floor surrounded by different seating areas. Some areas featured deep purple couches around tables topped with lit candles. There were also booths built into the walls, blocked by gauzy curtains for privacy.

Even though it was relatively early for the club scene, the place was already almost packed. People had already started to crowd onto the couches, talking in low tones. A deejay sat in a glass-enclosed room over the dance floor, while dancers grooved to the techno music he was spinning.

"Let's see if we can sit in one of those booths with the curtains," AJ suggested. "That way we can keep a watch for Holly. I'm not sure why she asked to meet us alone, at midnight. I'd rather not be seen until we know what's up."

Aly agreed, and the two found an empty booth. The filmy curtains gave them the ability to see out while making it hard for others to see inside. They couldn't help grooving along to the music as they sat in their seats. Then the song ended and some of the dancers left the floor, while another wave of dancers hit the floor, ready for the new song. One of them was a slim blond woman who bounced along to the beat, dancing wildly. Her long blond hair swung in the air.

"Isn't that—"AJ started.

"Calista?" Aly finished.

It was. The pop sensation was dancing away at Club Constellation.

"She doesn't look sick at all," AJ remarked. "If Calista is here, I wonder if Cadence is, too?"

Aly scanned the room. She spotted Cadence sitting by herself at a table in the corner of the room.

"She sure is," Aly said. "Should we even bother to say hello?"

"We might as well be polite," AJ said. "Anyway, something strange is going on with those two. I have to admit, I'm kind of curious."

Aly and AJ walked through the crowded club toward Cadence's table. Once again, she was chatting on her pink cell phone.

"But Calista, you really need to come back," they overheard Cadence say into the phone. She sounded stressed out.

AJ glanced at the dance floor. Calista was still out there, bopping to the beat. And she was not talking on the phone. Aly noticed, too. She looked at AJ and raised an eyebrow. This was strange.

Cadence looked up and spotted them. "I've got to go," she said into the phone and quickly put it away.

"Oh, hi," she said.

"Cadence, how are you?" Aly asked.

"Fine. What brings you guys here?" Cadence asked.

"Just checking out the nightlife," AJ answered. "It's a shame about Hope and Faith's video, isn't it?"

"Hmm? Oh, yeah. It's too bad." Cadence appeared distracted. "I'm sorry, but you'll have to excuse me. I need to go to the restroom." She got up and walked off.

Aly groaned. "Another friendly chat with Cadence. What's up with her?"

Before AJ could answer, Holly tapped her on the shoulder.

"Can we please talk in one of the private booths?" she asked.

"Sure," AJ answered. They followed Holly to an empty booth. She held up the curtain for them as they slid in, then she sat next to them, closing the curtain.

Even though Holly wasn't decked out in her Hollywood glam gown anymore, she still looked gorgeous. She wore a baby-doll, blue, v-neck tank top with lace trim and sequined straps along with a black short skirt, tights, and over-the-knee high-heeled boots. Her long hair was pulled back in a low ponytail.

"Thanks for coming," she said. "I'm sorry I had to act all super-spy to drop the note in your bag, but I didn't want my sisters to know we were meeting."

"It's okay," Aly said. "So what's up?"

Holly took a deep breath. "I really hope what I'm about to say stays between us. You see, the pin you found is mine. I was in the studio the night the footage was stolen. But I had nothing to do with it! I was looking for Maxine."

"Faith and Hope's manager?" AJ asked.

Holly nodded. "Yes. I want to start a solo career and I'm looking for a new manager. But I don't want my sisters to know. Not yet, anyway."

"Did Maxine see you there?" Aly asked.

"No. She wasn't there. I had made up some excuse and told my sisters I'd meet them by the car. I hurried in, hoping I could find Maxine quickly and arrange a time for us to meet. But I couldn't find her. Sabrina and Eve were waiting for me and I heard them calling my name. It made me panic and I left the studio in a hurry. I must have dropped the pin then," Holly explained.

"How did you get in?" AJ asked.

"The front door was open," Holly answered. She leaned forward. "I want you both to know that I did not steal the tape. I would never do something like that."

"Did you see anyone else there?" AJ said.

Holly shook her head from side to side. "No. I was only there for a few minutes, so anyone could have been there before or after me. But I need to ask you guys a favor. Please keep this a secret. When I decide to go solo, my sisters need to hear it from me."

Aly and AJ exchanged glances.

"Of course, we won't tell anyone," Aly promised her.

"Don't worry, your secret is safe with us," AJ said.

Holly let out a big sigh. "Thanks. I appreciate it. And thanks again for meeting me so late. I've got to get going. We're still shooting the video and tomorrow is another early day."

Aly and AJ said good-bye and watched as Holly slid out of the booth and walked out of the club.

"Do you believe her when she says she had nothing to do with the disappearance of the tape?" AJ asked Aly.

"You know, I really do. I think Holly told us the truth," Aly said.

AJ nodded. "I do, too. But that doesn't mean Sabrina or Eve or maybe even both of them didn't take the tape! They still had the motive—and the opportunity." She frowned. "Holly said the door was open. Did Lionel leave it open by mistake?"

"Or maybe Holly came in after the thief. The thief picked the lock to get in, and left the door open on the way out," Aly suggested. She stood up. "Enough mysteries. Let's dance!" Then she grabbed AJ's hand and dragged her out of the booth.

They hit the floor just as a funky dance tune began to play. Swaying to the beat, Aly and AJ forgot about the troubles of the day and began to have fun.

They had danced through the song and right into the next when Calista danced up next to them, smiling.

"Hey, guys," she shouted over the music.

Aly and AJ began to dance with Calista. They were joking and laughing. But after a few more songs, they were thirsty. Aly and AJ left the dance floor and sat at a table. Calista followed them and sat down next to them.

After ordering some water from the waitress, AJ turned to Calista.

"How are you feeling?" she asked.

"What?" Calista looked confused for a moment. "Oh, a lot better, thanks for asking," she said.

"Does this mean you'll be able to reshoot Faith and Hope's video?" Aly wondered.

Calista's bright smile dimmed. "I don't know about that. Cadence can be a little bossy. I'm lucky I got to come here tonight. But I was just dying to go out and have some fun, you know?"

AJ scanned the room for Cadence. She was

nowhere in sight. It seemed like Calista was more willing to talk without her sister around.

Aly smiled at Calista. "I don't want to start gushing again, but I really did love *Fun House* when I was growing up. My favorite part was the magic tricks, especially when you would make Boo Bunny appear out of the hat." She laughed. "I really thought you guys were magic. I was wondering how you learned to do those tricks at such a young age. Was it hard to learn?"

"That was all Cadence," Calista said. "She loved learning the magic tricks and she was a whiz at getting out of handcuffs. That's how she could do all the escape tricks."

"Did I hear my name?" Cadence asked. She stood over the table, clutching her phone in one hand and her purse in the other.

Calista looked startled. "Cadence! I was just telling Aly and AJ about the magic tricks you used to do on the show."

Cadence smiled. "That was my favorite part. I used to spend hours practicing some of those tricks. But Calista, it is getting late. We really need to get home."

Calista frowned. "Fine. Let's go."

"Good night," Cadence said. Calista nodded as she got up and left with her sister.

AJ glanced at her watch. "Wow! It's late. We probably should get going, too."

The deejay began to play a new song. It was "Potential Breakup Song," a song from Aly and AJ's album *Insomniatic.*

Aly smiled. "You know we've got to dance to this one!"

They hit the floor, grooving out to their song. AJ felt a tap on her shoulder. It was a girl in a silver minidress, dancing with a boy with spiky brown hair.

"Is it really you?" the girl asked, still dancing. "I mean, your song is playing, and you're here, like, dancing. That's wild!"

Her dance partner nodded. "Great song."

"Thanks!" Aly and AJ replied. It felt great to see people dancing to their music. After the song ended they kept on dancing until finally they were too beat to keep going.

"That was fun!" Aly exclaimed as they left the club.

"A blast!" AJ agreed. "But look, the sun is rising. These Nashville nights are getting to be exhausting!"

CHAPTER EIGHT:
A NIGHT AT THE OPRY

"All right, I've got to know," their mom, Carrie, said. "Why are you two still wearing your sunglasses? We're indoors."

Aly and AJ had only gotten a few hours of sleep when their alarm clock rang. They'd promised to go sightseeing with their mom that morning, and didn't want to disappoint her. They were in the art gallery in the Parthenon, a replica of a beautiful ancient Greek building right in the heart of Nashville.

"Promise not to lecture," Aly said. She removed her sunglasses to reveal pretty green eyes—with dark circles under them.

Carrie shook her head. "Not you, too, Amanda?"

AJ took off her glasses, too, showing the same tired eyes.

"We went out dancing at Club Constellation, and we just got a little . . . carried away," AJ said.

"The deejay was off the hook," Aly added.

"You two are in the middle of a big tour!" Carrie scolded. "You need to rest, not dance the night away."

"Mom, you promised not to lecture," Aly said.

Carrie frowned. "Actually, I didn't."

"Oh, right," Aly said. "Okay, how about we promise to go to sleep early tonight. Right after . . ."

"Right after what?" Carrie asked suspiciously.

"Right after we go see Faith and Hope perform

at the Grand Ole Opry tonight," AJ jumped in. "They texted us last night with the invite. We had to say yes!"

"It's the most famous country music show in the world," Aly pointed out.

Carrie softened a little. "The Grand Ole Opry. I can see how you wouldn't want to miss that. Did you know that its first live radio show aired in 1925?"

"I did some reading up on it," AJ said. "Some of the greatest acts in country music history have performed live at the Grand Ole Opry. Elvis Presley performed there for the first time when he was around our age."

"The show starts at 7:30, and we'll go to the hotel right after," Aly promised. "No dancing."

"I suppose that's fine," Carrie said. "But maybe you two should take a little nap this afternoon. Just to refresh yourselves."

Now it was Aly's turn to shake her head. "Mom, we are not little kids!"

"It's just a suggestion," Carrie said.

They continued to look at the paintings in the art museum. Then they moved to the main hall of the building, where a giant statue of the Greek goddess Athena stood.

"Wow," Aly remarked. The statue stood forty feet tall and was covered in gold.

Aly took out her camera. "Mom, AJ, stand in front," she directed. "That way we can see how big it really is."

Aly snapped a few pictures.

"This is a really cool place," AJ remarked. "It's like being in ancient Greece, but we're right here in Nashville."

"You know, there's a really good barbeque restaurant just next door," Carrie said. "We can get some ribs and eat them here in the park."

"Sounds great!" Aly and AJ agreed.

It was a bright sunny day, and Aly and AJ put on their sunglasses once again as they headed outside. They bought some ribs and ate them under the shadow of the Parthenon.

"So, Jim told me that the master tape of Faith and Hope's video was stolen," Carrie began as they ate. "That's such a shame! Why would somebody do such a thing?"

"We think maybe someone wants to ruin Faith and Hope's big moment at the music awards," AJ said.

"At first we thought it was one of the sisters from HeavenSent," Aly explained. "We found one of their logo pins in the studio. But Holly from HeavenSent says the pin is hers, and she swears she didn't steal the tape."

"My, you two sound just like detectives," Carrie said. "Come to think of it, every stop on this tour has had some kind of mystery in store. How strange."

"This might be the strangest stop of all," AJ went on. "Cadence and Calista were in the video with us. But they won't reshoot the video because they claim Calista is sick. But we saw Calista last night at the club. She looked fine."

"And then we heard Cadence talking on the cell phone to Calista, only Calista wasn't talking on *her* cell phone," Aly added. "It doesn't make sense at all."

"Do you think they have something to do with the stolen tape?" Carrie asked.

AJ looked thoughtful. "I hadn't thought of that. I can't see why they would want to steal the tape, because they agreed to be in it. But they're definitely acting suspicious. And they didn't go out to dinner with the rest of us. So they would have had a chance to break into the studio room, if they wanted to."

Aly yawned. "I am beat! You know, taking a nap doesn't sound like such a bad idea after all."

Carrie grinned. "I'll get the car. Let's head back to the hotel."

Three hours later, Aly and AJ were rested, showered, and getting ready to go out.

"I've always wanted to go to the Grand Ole Opry House," Aly said as she studied the clothes hanging on the rack in the hotel room. "Some really awesome musicians have played there."

She took a silky black camisole from the rack, along with a ruffled black skirt. She held them out to AJ. "What do you think?" she asked.

AJ nodded. "I was thinking of doing black, too," she said. She picked up a black-and-white patterned minidress with spaghetti straps.

"Cool," Aly said. "I like it when we match."

"Although we should probably avoid dressing exactly alike," AJ pointed out. "That would just be creepy."

"It was cute when Cadence and Calista used to do it," Aly said.

AJ nodded. "True. But they're obviously different people with different tastes now."

Aly frowned. "I'm not sure 'different' is better. I thought they would be so nice!"

"Well, Faith and Hope are nice," AJ reminded her. "We'd better hurry so we're not late for their show."

Jim had arranged for a car to take them to the Grand Ole Opry House. The girls stepped out into the warm summer night. Lights illuminated the two-story building, which looked almost like an old-fashioned theater. Huge chandeliers glowed through the large windows on the second floor. On top of the roof, large lit-up letters spelled out GRAND OLE OPRY HOUSE.

"How cool!" Aly remarked.

"I read that the Opry show has been held here since 1974," AJ said. "The show started out in a radio studio, and it got so popular they had to keep moving to bigger and bigger auditoriums."

Aly looked up at the lights. "It's like walking into a piece of history."

"We should head to the box office," AJ said. "Faith said our tickets would be waiting for us there."

They walked toward the entrance of the concert hall. There was a sudden commotion at the front door.

"You can't keep me out! I paid for my ticket!" a man was screaming. Two security guards held his arms, and were dragging him outside.

"As we've told you, sir, the Walker Sisters have a restraining order against you," one of the guards said. "You can leave quietly, or we can call the police and have you arrested."

AJ gasped. "That's Parker Mackenzie!"

"Boy, he likes to make a scene wherever he goes, doesn't he?" Aly remarked.

They watched as Parker broke away from the guards and walked away in a huff. He climbed into a small red sports car and sped away.

"Hey, we've seen that car before," Aly

realized. "It's the same one Jim liked the night he brought us to the studio."

"The same night the tape was stolen," AJ said. She shook her head. "We totally forgot about Parker as a suspect! He's so angry with Faith and Hope for firing him. He might have stolen the tape for revenge. We need to interview him."

"Right now, we need to see Faith and Hope sing," Aly reminded her. "We can deal with Parker later."

Faith and Hope had given them front-row tickets for the show. Aly and AJ smiled when the sisters came onstage, looking happy and relaxed. They were backed by a drummer, a guitarist, a fiddle player, and a banjo player. The sisters launched into their set of country songs, singing together in perfect harmony. When they sang "Nothing Like a Sister," Aly and AJ stood up and cheered.

When their set was over, Aly and AJ headed backstage to thank Faith and Hope for the tickets. They found Faith and Hope in their dressing room, looking tired but happy.

"That was a fantastic show!" Aly said.

"Thanks so much for inviting us," AJ added.

"You're welcome," Faith said. "You know, when we're up there singing, it's like everything else melts away. I'm so happy onstage."

"It shows," Aly said.

Hope stood up and stretched. "Singing also makes me soooo hungry! Do y'all want to go out for a bite to eat?"

Aly and AJ looked at each other. They had promised their mom they wouldn't stay out late.

"But it's just for a bite to eat," Aly said, reading AJ's mind.

"And we did have a nap today," AJ added. "I don't feel tired at all."

"Then you have to go out with us!" Faith prodded.

Aly and AJ grinned. "Well, when you put it that way, let's go!"

CHAPTER NINE:
A CLOSE CALL

Aly and AJ didn't totally dismiss their mom's advice. They made sure they were back at the hotel by midnight.

"This is an early night for us in Nashville," AJ joked.

They slept late the next day and ate brunch at the hotel. AJ's cell phone rang. It was Hope. AJ put her on speakerphone.

"Good news—sort of," she told AJ. "The record

company is going to give us the money to reshoot the video. We're still not sure if the music awards will air it without Cadence and Calista in it. But Maxine's working on them. That gal could sell sand to a man living in the desert, so we think we have a good chance."

"That's great!" Aly said.

"We were wondering if you two could meet with us this afternoon at the studio," Hope continued. "We have some new ideas, and we'd love to get your input."

"We're there," Aly said. "What time?"

"Two o'clock," Hope answered. "Thanks so much! You two are the best."

Aly hung up the phone.

"I'm glad things are working out."

Aly and AJ looked up to see Jim standing by their table. He had heard the phone conversation with Hope.

"Me too," Aly said. "Although I still wish we knew who had stolen that tape."

"Hey, we forgot all about interviewing Parker Mackenzie," AJ said. "We should try to do that today."

"Listen, you guys only have a few more days in Nashville, so take some time to relax and have fun," Jim advised. "Once we're back on the Hello Kitty bus, it'll be nothing but days of interviews and publicity. There are a lot of cool things to see in Nashville. Did you know that Gibson makes its electric guitars here?"

Aly's eyes widened. "Is there a factory tour?"

Jim shook his head. "Not in Nashville, but I hear the retail store is amazing."

That was all Aly and AJ needed to hear. They could spend hours looking at guitars—especially Gibsons, some of the most famous guitars in the world.

AJ looked at her watch. "We have to meet Faith and Hope in three hours. That should be plenty of time."

Jim grinned. "Great! I could use a little fun myself."

Twenty minutes later they were surrounded by racks of gleaming electric guitars.

"Each guitar is hand-painted in the factory," Aly said, admiring one with a bright electric-blue finish.

AJ was distracted by a wall lined with guitars painted in all different designs. One caught her eye—a black guitar with colorful swirls and flowers painted on the body. The bottom of the body was cut out in a v-shape.

"No way," AJ said, walking closer. "Is that what I think it is?"

Jim and Aly walked up next to her. "The Psychedelic Flying V," Jim read from a sign. "Hey, that's Jimi Hendrix's guitar!"

"It's a limited edition," AJ said, her eyes shining. "That is truly awesome."

"I really like that one," Aly said. She pointed to

a guitar with a soft silver paint job, covered with a cascade of flowers.

"I think you have a shirt that would match that," AJ joked.

A salesclerk in a Gibson guitar T-shirt walked up to them.

"Hey, it's Aly and AJ," he said. He was about twenty years old, with a mop of blond hair, green eyes, and a Southern drawl. "My name's Tyler. It'd be great if y'all would play something for us."

Aly grinned. "Just show us where to plug in!"

Tyler hooked them up with two guitars from the floor: the electric-blue one for Aly and a bright red one for AJ. They plugged into two amps, tuned up, and then launched into "Bullseye," a track from their *Insomniatic* album. A small crowd gathered around as they played.

Aly and AJ smiled at each other as they played. Playing in front of thousands of people was great, but it was just as much fun playing in front of ten people.

They ended the song to a round of applause.

"Y'all sure can rock out," Tyler said, grinning. "I hope y'all are havin' a good time here in Nashville."

"Definitely," Aly said. "But we've been here more than a week and we don't have any souvenirs yet."

"I can help you with that," Tyler said. He helped the girls pick out a Gibson guitar T-shirt for each of them. Then he showed them a case full of necklaces with different Gibson guitars. Aly and AJ each picked out one that they liked. Jim got himself a denim jacket with the Gibson logo on the front.

The time at the Gibson store passed quickly. They said good-bye to Tyler, and Jim drove them to Nashville Star Studios. They sat around a table with Faith, Hope, Maxine, and Lionel.

"Thanks for coming," Lionel said, beginning the meeting. "I'm really excited about reshooting the video. I think it will be even better than before.

Faith, why don't you tell everyone what you and Hope have in mind."

"Sure," Faith said. "First of all, we loved Aly and AJ's scenes with Brady and Michael. So we're going to bring them back."

Aly smiled, remembering the cute models. "That's *totally* fine with us!"

"And we still have the stuff from the shopping scene, so Hope and I are going to use it instead of Cadence and Calista this time," Faith said. "We just need to think of a way to bring the 'sister' angle in."

"I thought we could just try on a bunch of cute clothes," Hope suggested.

AJ's eyes brightened. "I know! What if one of you is trying on some hideous outfits, and the other sister saves the day with really cute clothes?"

Lionel laughed. "That could be really funny."

"And I hate to admit it, but it's not too far from the truth," Faith said. "Hope is always saving me from fashion disasters."

Aly was getting into the idea, too. "In the end of the scene, you could put on the outfits that you're wearing to your concert."

"Perfect," Lionel said. "Then we can cut to Aly and AJ running to get to your concert, and then show Faith and Hope on stage."

Faith looked happy. "That's really good!"

"I like this idea a lot," Maxine said. "It will show your fans how adorable you both are."

Faith and Hope blushed.

"Thanks, Maxine," Faith said. "But do you think the National Music Awards will still air it?"

Maxine winked. "Don't you worry about a thing, sugars. I'm working on it."

"Aly and AJ, can you film on Friday?" Lionel asked.

AJ nodded. "Sure. That's our last day in Nashville."

"And it'll be done just in time for the music awards," Faith said. "Thanks so much!"

Lionel stood up. "Fantastic, everyone. I'll see you all Friday morning, six A.M. sharp."

Aly and AJ walked out of the studio with Faith and Hope.

"I guess we'll be going to sleep early Thursday night," Aly remarked. "It's time to say good-bye to our Nashville nights."

"There's always tonight," Hope said, her eyes twinkling with mischief.

"Very tempting," AJ said. "I was thinking maybe we should do some clothes shopping first. We could find some hideous outfits for the video shoot."

"I've been so worried about the tapes, it feels like I haven't done anything fun in years," Faith said. "We'd love to go."

"We'll drive with the top down on the convertible," Hope promised.

"Sounds great!" Aly exclaimed, and AJ nodded in agreement.

The girls walked outside the studio and followed

Faith and Hope across the studio parking lot. Suddenly, a squeal of brakes pierced the air.

Faith and Hope froze, terrified. Aly and AJ turned to see a red sports car speeding through the parking lot. It was aimed right at the Walker Sisters!

"Faith! Hope! Look out!" AJ screamed.

Aly grabbed Hope by the arm, and AJ grabbed Faith. They pulled them back just in time, as the speeding red car barreled past them. They quickly ran back to the safety of the building.

Faith's face was pale white, and Hope was crying.

"What—what just happened?" Faith asked.

CHAPTER TEN:
NABBED!

Faith and Hope hugged each other, shaking. Aly and AJ exchanged glances. They had both recognized the car—it belonged to Parker Mackenzie.

"Let's go inside and sit down," AJ suggested.

Maxine was running toward the front door when they came in. "I heard all the yelling. What happened out there?"

"Parker Mackenzie tried to hit Faith and

Hope with his car," AJ said. Maxine went pale.

Hope sniffled. "He would have hit us, too, if Aly and AJ hadn't pulled us out of the way."

"This is very serious," Maxine said. "I am going to call the police right now. Are you sure it was Parker?"

Aly nodded. "It was his car."

Maxine disappeared for a few moments, and the girls went into one of the studio rooms and sat down. The Walker Sisters' manager appeared a few minutes later.

"The police will be here in a moment," she said. "They'll be escorting you girls down to the police station to give a report. Aly and AJ, they'll need to hear what you have to say."

Aly and AJ nodded. "No problem," Aly said. "I'm just glad that everyone is okay."

"Maxine, we think Parker might have stolen the tape, to get revenge on Faith and Hope," AJ said. "Is it okay if we let the police know about that?"

Maxine nodded. "Tell them everything. I don't care about bad publicity. Faith and Hope's safety is the most important thing."

They spent the rest of the afternoon with the police. An officer came to the studio and took statements from everyone. Officer Hill was a tall, graying man with kind, blue eyes. After he took their statements, he asked them to go down to the police station.

"This is a serious crime," he told them. "If what you say is true, Faith and Hope could have been seriously injured, or worse. We want to make sure you're safe until we can locate Mr. Mackenzie and determine what happened."

Luckily, the time at the police station passed quickly. The officers on duty were sympathetic about what had happened, but they were also thrilled to have two sets of sister singing sensations in the station. Aly, AJ, Faith, and Hope signed autographs while they waited for some news.

After about two hours, Officer Hill came to see them.

"We have Mr. Mackenzie in custody," he told them. "Besides your statements, we interviewed some other people in the area who saw his car speed out of the parking lot. We've got enough evidence to hold him right now. We're also getting a search warrant for his apartment, so we can see if he has that stolen tape in his possession."

"Thank you so much," Faith said. Her voice sounded tired. She gave Aly and AJ a sad smile. "Sorry we didn't get to go shopping."

"Don't even worry about it," Aly said. "You're safe and Parker's in custody. That's the main thing."

"Just go home and get some rest," AJ said. "I know that's what we're going to do."

Faith and Hope squeezed the sisters in big hugs. "You two are like our guardian angels, honest," Hope said. "I don't know what we'd have done without you."

"We'll see you on Friday morning," Aly said. "Call us if you need us, okay?"

Faith and Hope nodded. Aly and AJ walked outside to find Jim waiting for them.

"I have strict orders from your mom to bring you back to the hotel," he said.

Aly and AJ gratefully climbed into the car. The whole incident had left them drained.

"No argument here," Aly said. "We're not going anywhere tonight."

As soon as they got back to the hotel, Aly and AJ each took a hot bubble bath, climbed into their pajamas, and ordered room service. Soon they were sprawled out on their beds with Caesar salads and ice cream sundaes. Aly picked up the TV remote.

"Let's watch a movie," she suggested. "I just need to veg out for a while."

"Excellent idea," AJ agreed. "See what's on the movie channel."

Aly scanned through the movie titles on the screen. She stopped at one titled *Cat Burglar.*

"Ooh, I wanted to see that!" she cried. "A police detective falls in love with this mysterious woman, but he doesn't know that she's a cat burglar robbing all the rich people in town. It's action-packed and romantic at the same time."

"Let's do it," AJ said. She dimmed the lights in the room, and Aly ordered the movie.

They watched, talking back at the screen like they had since they were kids.

"Ooh! I want that dress she's wearing!"

"How can he not know she's the cat burglar? He's not stupid!"

"There's no way she'll get away with it!"

At one part in the film, Jade, the cat burglar, recruited two women to help her with a big jewelry heist. AJ shrieked and pointed at the screen.

"Hey, that's Sabrina from HeavenSent!" she cried.

"That's right!" Aly said. "I read she was trying to start a movie career. I wonder if she's any good?"

"Ssshhh. She's on!" AJ hissed.

Sabrina was dressed in a tight leather jumpsuit, her dark hair in a long braid down her back. She walked up to the back door of a museum in the moonlight. Then she opened a metal canister hanging around her neck and took out something that looked like a lock pick. She began to pick the lock on the door.

"Pause it! Pause it!" AJ screamed.

Aly used the remote to pause the film. "What's the emergency? Bathroom break?"

"No, silly!" AJ said. "Look at Sabrina!"

Aly looked at the screen. "Yeah, she's picking a lock."

"Exactly!" AJ said. "And the person who stole the video had to pick a lock to get to it."

"But this is just a movie," Aly pointed out.

"She's not picking the lock for real."

"Maybe not, but actors always learn how to do things for real to make movies more realistic," AJ said. "Like sword fighting and stuff. Maybe Sabrina took a lock-picking lesson to get ready for her role."

AJ grabbed her notebook from the nightstand and began to write furiously.

"You're right," Aly agreed. "But I'm pretty sure Parker Mackenzie is the one who stole the tape, don't you think?"

AJ put down her pen. "Oh, right," she said. "I guess so. But we won't know for sure until the police search his apartment. If he didn't do it, then I say Sabrina is a good suspect. HeavenSent still has the best motive."

"Agreed," Aly said. "But as far as we know, the police are handling things now. Can't we just watch the movie and forget about being detectives for a while?"

"Fine," AJ said, but Aly noticed she still held her pen and notebook.

Aly fell back against her pillows, laughing. "You are hopeless!" she teased.

Hope

CHAPTER ELEVEN:
CAUGHT IN THE ACT

The phone in their hotel room rang the next morning. AJ answered it.

It was Faith. "Parker Mackenzie is still in jail," she told AJ. "But the police searched his apartment, and didn't find the tape. They say Parker claims he didn't steal it. He didn't even know it was missing."

"How are you feeling today?" AJ asked.

"Still a little shaken up," Faith admitted.

"Hope and I are going to take it easy today. We want to look good for the video shoot tomorrow."

"Good idea," AJ said. "Aly and I are pretty excited about tomorrow. We'll see you in the morning."

AJ hung up the phone as Aly walked out of the bathroom, drying her hair with a towel.

"I was thinking maybe we could try to go to the guitar factory again today," she said. Then she noticed the serious expression on her sister's face. "What's up?"

"Parker Mackenzie didn't steal the tape," AJ told her. "The police searched his house."

Aly shrugged. "Okay. But the video is being reshot. So everything's turned out all right in the end, hasn't it?"

"But it's not the end yet," AJ pointed out. "The National Music Awards might not even air the new video. And we know that someone was trying to sabotage Faith and Hope. What if they mess with the video reshoot somehow? I'd feel better if we knew who did it, and why."

Aly sighed. "I guess you're right. I'd hate to reshoot the whole video for no reason. Faith and Hope would be crushed."

AJ opened her notebook. "The way I see it, Sabrina and Eve are still suspects because they have a motive. Sabrina is a bigger suspect than Eve, because she might have learned how to pick locks when she filmed *Cat Burglar*."

"Right," Aly agreed. "And Cadence and Calista are suspects, too, because they've been acting so weird. Plus, they had the opportunity to steal the tape. They just don't have a motive, as far as we can see."

"Maybe we should split up," AJ said. "I'm really curious about Cadence and Calista. Maybe I can talk to them, and you can talk to Sabrina."

"Sounds good," Aly said. "Now all we need

to do is track down three super-mega celebrities and get private meetings with them. That should be easy."

"Ah, but we have a secret weapon," AJ reminded her. She held up her cell phone.

Aly was confused for a minute, but then she got it. "Jim!"

AJ dialed the number. "Jim, are you busy? Aly and I need a little favor . . ."

Three hours later Aly sat in the back of a taxicab, driving through downtown Nashville. Jim had really come through. He'd made a call to one of HeavenSent's personal assistants and charmed the girls' schedule out of her. He'd learned that Sabrina had a lunch date at Rush, a trendy eatery nestled between funky shops in a strip of brick buildings. Aly noticed a sweet pair of jeans in a shop window and made a mental note to check them out on her way back.

Hey, focus, Alyson, she scolded herself. *You've got important work to do here. Faith and Hope are counting on you.*

She had spent the last hour figuring out what to say to Sabrina. Should she pretend their meeting was a coincidence? Should she boldly accuse her of stealing the tape, and see if she admitted it? She still wasn't sure.

"Guess I'll have to wing it," she muttered as the cab pulled up in front of the restaurant.

She paid the driver and stepped out into the Nashville heat. She walked into the restaurant, a cozy place with small tables and brightly colored abstract paintings of city buses and cars on the walls. She scanned the room and saw Sabrina in the corner, facing the door. Her hair was pulled back in a scarf, and she wore dark sunglasses. She was talking to a man whose back was to Aly.

Here goes nothing, Aly thought. She walked

toward Sabrina and saw the singer gasp when she spotted Aly.

"Okay, Aly," Sabrina said, taking off her sunglasses. "You've got me! I'm guilty!"

CHAPTER TWELVE:
STILL A PUZZLE

"You stole the master tape of Faith and Hope's video?" Aly asked. Getting a confession had been easier than she thought!

Sabrina looked puzzled. "Tape? What are you talking about?"

Now Aly was confused, too. "Well, you said you were guilty . . ."

Sabrina shook her head. "Oh, great! I just gave myself up for no reason." She pointed to the man in front of her. "Aly, meet JB Rawlings."

The man in the chair turned around and gave Aly a bright smile. He wore a stylish blue silk suit and gold chains around his neck.

JB stood up and extended a hand to Aly. He slipped a business card into her hand. "Pleasure to meet you. You and your sister are very talented. If you're ever looking for a new manager, give me a call."

Suddenly, everything made sense to Aly. Sabrina wearing sunglasses and a scarf. Meeting a talent manager in a restaurant . . . without her sisters.

"I get it," Aly said. "You're looking for a new manager. And you don't want your sisters to know." *Just like Holly,* Aly added to herself.

"It's true," Sabrina said. "I'm tired of being known as 'one of those girls from HeavenSent.' Most people don't even get our names right. It's time for me to step into the spotlight."

JB nodded. "That's right where you're going, baby. Just leave it to me."

Sabrina gave Aly a pleading look. "Please don't tell anybody! JB and I are finalizing our deal. I'll let my sisters know when I'm ready. I know they'll be shocked. I just want to spare them any extra pain, if I can."

"Your secret's safe with me," Aly said. "But maybe you shouldn't worry so much. Your sisters might not be as shocked as you think. I can usually figure out what's going on in my sister AJ's head, even if she won't talk to me about it."

"Thanks," Sabrina said, smiling warmly. "I'd ask you to sit with us, but . . ."

"No problem," Aly said, thinking of the jeans she'd seen in the shop window. "I've got some shopping to do, anyway."

While Aly tracked down Sabrina, AJ was on

a mission of her own. Getting through to Cadence and Calista's people had taken Jim a little bit longer, but finally, he'd come through. He knew which hotel they were staying in, and their room number. It was up to AJ to figure out how to get in to see the famous sisters.

AJ had devised part of a plan. She'd bought a small teddy bear in the hotel gift shop. She would knock on the door and say she was there to see how Calista was feeling. She doubted it would work—the sisters had not been very friendly—but she had to try something.

AJ took the elevator up to the hotel's top floor and hit the buzzer on Calista and Cadence's room.

To AJ's surprise, the door opened right away. It was Cadence. Her bobbed hair looked like it hadn't been combed, and she wore a white tank top and ripped jeans.

"Oh, it's you," she said. "I was expecting someone else."

AJ held out the teddy bear. "Aly and I just want to say we're hoping Calista is feeling better. Is she here?"

"Calista? Oh, she's at the doctor now. He's checking her out," Cadence answered.

AJ took a bold step into the room. "Then let me just leave this teddy bear for her," she said, talking quickly. She had a feeling Cadence was going to kick her out any second. "It's a shame Calista's not feeling well. Aly and I are going to reshoot the video with Faith and Hope tomorrow. We had so much fun the first time. It's a shame you two can't do it."

"Yeah, whatever," Cadence said with a shrug. "Listen, I don't mean to be rude, but—"

There was a knock on the open door. A man in a navy hotel uniform stood there.

"Ms. Collins? You have a package?"

Cadence picked up a large manila envelope from on top of the bedspread. "Yes, the concierge said you could send this overnight mail for me."

Curious, AJ glanced at the envelope as Cadence handed it to the man. It was addressed to Calista Collins. But what surprised AJ was that it was being sent to an address in Montana.

AJ's mind raced. Why was Cadence sending a package to her sister, if Calista was here in Nashville with her? Was Calista really at the doctor? Or was there some simple explanation? Maybe the sisters had an aunt named Calista who lived in Montana. It wasn't unusual for people to be named after relatives.

AJ was lost in thought when she noticed Cadence staring at her. "Listen, AJ, it's nice of you to bring the bear and everything, but I'm kind of busy right now."

"Oh, sure," AJ said. But she didn't want to give up so soon. "Do you think I should wait for Calista to get back so I can give her the bear myself?"

"Uh, no, I don't think you should wait," Cadence said, a little curtly. "I'll make sure she gets it."

Cadence practically pushed AJ out the door. AJ watched the door shut behind her and frowned.

I could wait in the hotel lobby until Calista gets back, AJ thought, but something told her that would be a waste of time. After all, she and Aly knew Calista wasn't really sick, so Cadence was lying about her being at the doctor. She didn't know where Calista was. Had she taken a quick flight to Montana? Is that why Cadence was sending her a package?

AJ shook her head. It didn't make sense. She felt like she was holding pieces to a puzzle, and she just couldn't put them together.

The video shoot was early tomorrow morning. They still didn't know who had stolen the master tape. Someone could try to sabotage Faith and Hope again.

And there was nothing she and Aly could do to stop it.

CHAPTER THIRTEEN:
THE MARK OF GUILT

Aly and AJ had agreed to meet at a Mexican restaurant on Music Row. Aly was already waiting at a table when AJ arrived.

"How did things go with Sabrina?" AJ asked.

"Well, I got a confession, but not the one I was hoping for," Aly began. She explained that Sabrina was trying to get a new manager in secret—just like her sister Holly.

"If Sabrina and Holly are looking for solo

careers, then the Walkers' sister act is not a threat," AJ reasoned. "I believe both of them. That just leaves Eve."

"Something tells me that if Sabrina and Holly are ready to split, Eve probably is, too," Aly guessed. "I'm thinking that HeavenSent aren't on the top of our suspect list anymore. What about Cadence and Calista?"

Before AJ could answer, a waitress came up to the table.

"Are you ready to order?"

"I'll have a taco platter and an iced tea," Aly said.

"I'll have the same, please," AJ added.

The waitress smiled, took their menus, and walked away.

"So, now that our order's out of the way, what did you find out?" Aly asked. "Did you get into the room?"

AJ nodded. "I did, but it was weird. Cadence

was alone, and said Calista was at the doctor. But I'm pretty sure she was lying. She only opened the door for me because she thought I was from the hotel, picking up a package. Then it gets even weirder. The package was addressed to Calista—in Montana."

"Montana?" Aly asked. "But I thought Cadence and Calista were staying in Nashville for a while?"

"Me too," AJ said. "It doesn't make sense. Those two are very suspicious. But I don't have any idea why they would want to steal the tape."

"Me either," Aly agreed. She leaned back in her seat. "Maybe this is one mystery we won't be able to figure out."

AJ took her notebook from her bag and began to leaf through the pages. "Don't say that. There's got to be something we overlooked. Aly, did you sketch anything that might be useful? Any clues?"

Aly took her sketchbook out of her bag. "I don't think so. I did a few quick sketches the day we filmed the video."

She turned to a page that showed Cadence and Calista in their sunglasses, pretending to shop for the video. "I sketched this before the tape was stolen, so I don't see how there could be a clue in it," she said. Then she frowned. "Hmm. That's strange."

"What's strange?" AJ asked.

Aly passed the sketchbook to her sister. "There's Cadence, with the short hair and the heart-shaped birthmark on her shoulder. But I forgot to draw a birthmark on Calista. Only, I'm thinking maybe I *didn't* forget."

"But you must have forgotten," AJ reasoned. "Everybody knows that Cadence and Calista have identical heart-shaped birthmarks."

"Right," Aly said. "So if Calista doesn't have a birthmark, maybe she's not Calista."

"A Calista impostor?" AJ thought about this, and her green eyes started to shine. The pieces of the puzzle were starting to come together in her head. "We have to know for sure about that birthmark."

AJ picked up her cell phone and started dialing.

"Faith? It's AJ," she said. "Was somebody taking publicity photos at the shoot? Yes? Is there any way Aly and I could look at them? We think we might have finally figured out who stole the master tape."

Aly heard Faith's excited voice on the other line. "Great. We'll be there as soon as we can," AJ said. Then she stood up.

"Faith and Hope are going to meet us at Nashville Star Studios. The photos are there," she said.

"Great!" Aly grabbed her bag.

Just then, the waitress walked up, carrying a tray full of food.

"Um, could we please get that to go?" Aly asked.

Faith and Hope were eagerly waiting for them at the studio. Maxine was with them. She had a folder of photos with her.

"We just got the prints today," Maxine said. "What exactly do you girls need them for?"

"We need a photo of Cadence and Calista in their sundresses," AJ explained.

Maxine flipped through the photos. "We've got some good ones. They looked so pretty. It's such a shame they won't reshoot the video."

Maxine handed them three photos. In all of the photos, the twins' shoulders were facing the camera. Cadence clearly had a birthmark on her right shoulder. Calista did not.

"Aha!" AJ cried. She showed the photos to Faith, Hope, and Maxine. "Calista clearly doesn't have a birthmark in these photos, right?"

Faith picked up a photo. "No, she doesn't," she said. "That's odd. I thought both twins had the same birthmark."

"They do," AJ said. "But these girls aren't twins. That isn't Calista in the photo."

"It's not?" Hope asked.

"No, it's not," Aly confirmed. "Now everything makes sense. We know who stole your master tape, and why."

"Well, this is big news," Maxine said. "What exactly is going on?"

AJ slipped the photos into her bag. "We'll tell you on the road. We have to get to Cadence's hotel—fast!"

CHAPTER FOURTEEN:
A DOUBLE DECEPTION

AJ pushed the button on Cadence's hotel room door. Aly, Faith, Hope, and Maxine stood behind her.

They heard footsteps behind the door. Then Cadence's voice. "Please go away. I'm busy."

AJ held a photo from the video shoot up to the peephole in the door. "I think you're going to want to see this photo, Cadence. It's a photo of Calista. Oh, I mean, whoever is *pretending* to be Calista."

The door slowly opened.

"So, you figured it out," Cadence said. She looked miserable.

"Most of it," AJ replied. "Can we come in? I don't think you want to talk about this out here."

Cadence reluctantly led them into the hotel room.

"Aly's sketch of you and Calista at the video shoot was the final clue," AJ began. "She noticed that Calista didn't have a birthmark. So whoever filmed that video with you isn't your sister."

"That's why you stole the master tape of the video," Aly continued. "You realized that Calista was filmed without her sweater on. When the video came on, all of your fans would realize the birthmark was missing. Then you'd have to explain why you were using a double."

Cadence sank down on the bed and ran a hand through her hair. "It's my cousin Megan," Cadence said. "We're the same age, and we've always looked alike. She needed contacts, some hair extensions, and hair color—then she looked just like Calista. Except I forgot about the birthmark."

"I don't understand," Faith broke in. "Where is the real Calista? Is she all right?"

"Calista is off pursuing her *dreams*," Cadence said, in a voice that clearly showed she thought that was a silly thing to do. "She's tired of singing. She wants to be an artist and design clothes. So she holed up in a ranch in the middle of nowhere in Montana."

AJ smiled. It made sense now. When Cadence was speaking on the phone at the club, she was talking to the real Calista. *But Calista, you really need to come back.* And that package had been addressed to the real Calista, in Montana.

"So to keep your secret, you waited until everyone left the studio," AJ said. "You knew how to pick locks because you know how to do magic tricks. You picked the lock and stole the tape."

Maxine was shaking her head. "That seems awfully desperate, sugar. Why not let Calista do her thing, and have a sweet solo career of your own?"

"I don't WANT a solo career!" Cadence said, standing up. She was shaking with anger. "Calista and I have been performing together since we were babies. After we left that stupid TV show we could have faded away into oblivion, but we worked hard. We developed a multimillion-dollar pop act. Our fans want to see Cadence and Calista—not just plain Cadence. Or Cadence and *Megan*, for that matter. It's just not the same."

The hotel room door opened, and Megan—the fake Calista walked in.

"Oh, hey everybody," she said, looking surprised. "I was just—"

"It's okay, Megan, they know," Cadence said, flopping back on the bed.

Megan turned pale. "Oh, I'm so sorry," she said. "It was—it was Cadence's idea, and I didn't see the harm in it, and it's my fault that I took off my sweater, only I never thought we'd have to steal your tape, and then we burned it, and I—"

"You *burned* it!" Hope said in disbelief. She and Faith faced Cadence and Megan now, angry.

Megan nodded. "It was so important to Cadence," she said in a small voice. "If everyone finds out I'm fake, her whole life will be ruined."

Aly and AJ exchanged glances. Things were getting tense in the room.

"Should we get the police involved?" AJ whispered to Aly.

But Maxine took control. She put an arm around Faith and Hope. "Now sweethearts, don't get all flustered. I firmly believe that things always work out for the best, and this is one of those times. That new video is going to be better than the old one, by far. You'll see."

Faith and Hope just nodded. They were still stunned.

Maxine turned her attention to Cadence and Megan. "I understand that desperate women do desperate things. You're going to make it up to these girls by introducing the video live at the National Music Awards. 'Faith and Hope, our favorite new sister act.'"

"She's good," Aly whispered to AJ. "She reminds me of Mom."

"We'll do whatever you want," Megan said tearfully. But Cadence looked suspicious.

"So you're going to keep our secret?" she asked.

"Oh, no, honey. I don't believe in secrets," Maxine replied. "I think you two just need some good management to make this little act of yours work. You don't have a manager, do you?"

Cadence shook her head. "Calista and I fired ours when we turned eighteen. We don't trust them."

"But you just never met the right person,"

Maxine said, her voice like butter. She put her arm around Megan now. "Sugar, how do you feel about changing your name to Clarissa?"

CHAPTER FIFTEEN:
NOTHING LIKE A SISTER

"Nothing like a sister.

Helps you when you're down.

Knows just what you're thinking.

Can turn your life around . . ."

On Saturday afternoon, Aly and AJ sat in director's chairs and watched Faith and Hope sing their hit for the new video. Maxine sat next to them, smiling and tapping her foot on the ground.

The last notes of the song faded away.

"Cut!" Lionel yelled. "Great work, everybody. I just want to check this last round of footage before I let everyone go. We've only got a day to edit this thing—I need to make sure we've got what we need."

Faith and Hope walked off the set. They looked happy.

"Making videos is so much fun," Hope said.

"Maxine, you were right," Faith added. "This is definitely going to be better than the first one."

"I like this one better because it really shows off what you two can do," Maxine said. "We didn't need Cadence and Calista in this video at all."

AJ held a copy of the afternoon newspaper up. "Speaking of Cadence and Calista, you sure work fast, Maxine," she said. She turned to a page and began to read an article out loud. "'Megastar sisters Cadence and Calista will be making a special appearance at the National Music Awards Monday night. They will be introducing a brand-new video by hot new act the Walker Sisters, and rumor has it they have a special announcement of their own.'"

"Ooh, it sounds mysterious," Aly said.

Maxine leaned in. "Can y'all keep a secret?" she asked. Everyone nodded.

"Calista is flying out from Montana," she said. "Cadence and Megan are going to come out first and sing a few lines from a song. Then Calista will come out, and everyone will realize that there are *two* Calistas. Calista will explain that she's becoming a fashion designer, and she'll announce her replacement, *Clarissa*. Of course, Cadence and Clarissa will be wearing gorgeous dresses designed by Miss Calista herself."

Faith shook her head. "You are truly amazing," she said. She turned to Aly and AJ.

"I wish you guys could be at the music awards with us."

"We'd love to, but we have to head to the next stop on our tour," Aly explained. "We'll be watching on our Hello Kitty TV, though."

AJ pointed to the newspaper. "There's more gossip in here. Check this out: 'Rumor has it, Saturday will be the last performance by HeavenSent. The sisters are rumored to be seeking solo careers.'"

"Hmm," Maxine said. "That is true, although I didn't let the cat out of the bag on that one. Must have been Sabrina or Eve's new manager."

"So you're managing Holly, then?" Aly asked. "She told us she was going to talk to you."

Maxine nodded. "That girl's got major talent. All of those sisters do. I'm sure they'll all do well."

"Faith! Hope! I need you for a moment!" Lionel called.

The Walker Sisters headed off, followed by Maxine, and Aly and AJ stood up and stretched.

"This week went by so fast," Aly said. "I can't believe we found another mystery here in Nashville. It's weird."

"I'm used to it by now," AJ said. "What I can't believe is that we actually solved this mystery. I was ready to give up."

"You? Give up?" Aly teased. "No way."

"I couldn't have done it without you," AJ said. "Faith and Hope are right. There's nothing like a sister."

Aly looked around the studio. "It's our last night in Nashville. I guess we'd better get back to the hotel and pack."

"That would make Mom happy," AJ agreed.

"Did you girls say it's your last night in Nashville?"

Brady and Michael, the two models from the shoot, walked up to them.